The Mind
of a
Sleuth

L.B. Robbins

ISBN: 978-1-953048-70-7 (Paperback)
        978-1-953048-92-9 (E-book)

Writers' Branding
1800-608-6550
www.writersbranding.com
orders@writersbranding.com

Contents

Chapter 1

Sea Isle City

My name is Angellica Peterson and I live in the pretty postcard town of Sea Isle City. It lies about one half hour from Atlantic City, a beautiful resort town that visitors flock to in summer. The other three seasons it's a quiet picturesque community near to where my son is a minister of a Lutheran Church. My husband and I moved here from Bucks County to be near our only child. Now I live here alone.

Robert Senior and I were presbyterians, though we attended separate churches. I was the OP or orthadox and Robert Sr. was the PCA, or left handed side of the union. Our son avoided this quandary by attending a Lutheran seminary where he happily met and married his true love Ruth. After a sensible length of time they produced healthy twins Robert and Joseph, who were the apple of my eye.

The evening in question, I was embarking on a new quilt pattern, when the phone rang, abruptly disrupting the rhythm of my pattern. I usually did my artistic work evenings as friends who knew better didn't call, and I was prepared to ignore this intruder.

My sixth sense told me to answer it, so I did. It was Robert and he sounded upset, as only I could tell. He could be quite an actor, but not now. "Mom, I'd like to meet for lunch tomorrow." How very odd, he was not a lover of the occasional lunch. "I have something to tell you and I can't talk right now. "How about (his old stutter was back)… You choose."

I had no problem answering quickly. "Lets try Docks" (it was the only restaurant I knew how to find in Atlantic City, it was across from the boardwalk) and it was very elegant. My mood improved immediately. I wondered what the problem was and forced myself to put off all worrying until tomorrow. It was probably a minor problem and a touch of the flu.

The next day I played with my new perm, chose something moderate, but safely tasteful, in other words, I dressed for a ride in my new Town Car, always a treat for me. I pulled up to the valet parking and was very surprised to see Robert waiting for me at the door. Definitely there was a problem. We hurried inside and chose a table in the corner of the darkly paneled room.

I settled myself into the plush velvet seat and relaxed into the mood of old money, silent waiters and the illusive smell of sea food. As we both perused the large leather menu, I looked at the grey palor of my son's face and wondered. He peeked out from behind his menu and I noticed a face drained of all color. I also noted his hated cowlick had gone rogue on him, resembling a wild corkscrew.

I had no need to check the menu, but I pretended to do so, I chose the cobb salad with crab and waited with curiosity for the reason behind this meeting . As soon as we were alone, he said, "Mom, I'm so ashamed, I've been so foolish. It's that trust fund you set up for me. I've been a real idiot, I thought I could beat the odds against the poor interest rate, and it's gone.

'Yes gone. Have you told Ruth about it?' "Of course I didn't. You know Ruth, I'd be dead right now," he said dejectedly. I unfortunately had to agree.

He continued, "It would never be enough in ten years for two boys, eight semesters of college". I agreed, of course, I could add. "An opportunity came up to invest it in a mortgage for ten years at 6 percent interest, and I foolishly jumped on it. Now it's gone,"
he repeated, then proceeded to tell me about it.

This was how the story went. There was a loyal member of the church who, along with his family had been a loyal one for years. He had a talent for repairing appliances, carpentry and all kinds of construction, plumbing, gardening, a jack of all trades. My son and his family had moved into an older style of parsonage, with much need of work, as my son had never had an interest in these things. It was inevitable, Mr. Moyer spent much time with them. He was easy to talk to, and was apt to ask questions, showing a quick and easy mind. He was a trustee and Robert had no reason to doubt him.

One day he approached my son with a proposition. He said he had been waiting for years for the adjoining cottage to his home to become available, and just that thing had happened. His offer was for a six percent contract for 10 years for thirty thousand dollars. He told him to think about it for a while, but the house might not last on the market.

Robert had received a notice from the bank that the interest rate was being lowered on his variable rate trust and he took a ride by the little cottage. It was quaint, and true to Frank's words probably wouldn't last long on the market. Frank Moyer had been a faithful member for so long, so eager to help when needed. What could possibly go wrong?

He'd been assured that there would be legal paperwork, properly filed. When the mortgage appeared, he took some time to think about it. He was not pressured in any way except for the pure logic of it all. Robert signed the papers in the presence of a notary public at the bank. The big mistake he made was to tell Mr. Moyer his copy had been filed safely in the his lock box (he had no idea that Mr. Moyer was aware of the hidden fire box on the side of his fire place, as he had never shown it to anyone). Who could have known what would happen, he had nothing of value in it, as it was for purposes of fire only.

My mind went back to the faux ceramic fireplace his father and I had purchased in the French quarter in New Orleans, a nineteenth century antique, quite novel. It had a metal fire door on the side, which we'd always used to store valuable papers in, as it was hidden from view by a plant.

The family went on a small vacation and Robert, in his innocence had neglected to remove the spare key in the garage, not many people knew of it.

Robert had been assured the papers had been copied and filed with the courthouse. Now, Frank had disappeared, and the paperwork was missing! It had never been filed in the courthouse, as Frank had offered to do. It was the only document missing.

Robert hadn't touched his sandwich. He looked so young, all of a sudden, I wrapped the untouched sandwich for him, he just said "Thanks Mom" and started to leave. I could see the problem at once. He was supposed to be a good steward with a trustworthy record. Once bad judgment entered in, well, best not to think of what might happen.

When I reached home, I thought of how different our two marriages were. Had the same thing happed with his father and I, I would have been the first person he would have turned to! Unlike his son, he had been a stockbroker and wouldn't have been surprised at this strange turn of events.

Poor Robert had been so close mouthed about his trust but, as he confessed he had neglected to remove it from his desk when Mr. Moyer had been reinforcing a bookshelf in his study. Robert had answered a call in the kitchen at the time, leaving the culprit alone just long enough. Who thought a farmer would be interested in the details of a financial document.

When he'd returned he'd found Mr. Moyer glancing through a book on the missionary travels of Paul in the Greek Islands on his desk. The man seemed to be a sponge for knowledge of the gospel!

Until now, Robert had been proud of his new investment. Uncle Clovis, a beloved church member, would have had a place to move into, where he could be closely cared for and Frank Moyer would have a new, nice neighbor. A good plan for all three of them, or so Robert thought at the time, yes six percent!.

Not only had Robert's pride taken a downward spiral, but he was engaged with a potentially criminal personality and had to move carefully because of his position in the church. These devout Lutherans had known Robert for less than two years, but had been worshiping with the Moyer family for more than thirty. Move carefully indeed.

Chapter 2

Get to Work

I awoke the next morning with resolve to get involved with my new mission, to help my son restore some, part, or all of this trust fund which had been so brazenly removed from him by sheer craftiness. Someone had used his caring mind toward his parishioners, such as Uncle Clovis, to blindside him to invest his sound investment into the hands of a cold, calculating, sinister loner. The loner in question had a talent for repairing appliances, furniture and walls, a talent which had endearing himself to a few scattered influential people in town, my son included.

Time for a quick walk back in time. Two years ago I was the unlikely recipient of an inheritance, which was introduced by a surprised vision. I was so overwhelmed by the vision, I felt it necessary to write a short story about it, something I had never done before. The intention was to tell of God's goodness, but instead some of my more intimate sisters decided I had taken the opportunity to brag of new wealth and the story took in a new meaning. Unfortunately legal fees had eaten away the bulk of the estate.

What I was left with I shared with my son Robert in the form of a trust fund, a Town Car for myself and numerous requests for loans. It was as if stardom now had a new unfortunate consequence in the form of this new theft!

I reviewed the crime again, in the light of a new day. The fact that it was a premeditated crime was assented to by the theft from the home and the careful spying out of personal, financial statements in the quick minutes granted to him by the unexpected phone call. The man was very quick and alert, taking advantage of an opportunity which presented itself to him, "on the fly". He must have had a terrific need of money. My son had revealed that Mr. Moyer had lost his job at the casino in Atlantic City, but so had many others, and they hadn't resorted to any sort of criminal activity.

I checked out the membership directory that Robert had supplied me with and looked at the lightly ticked pencil marks of some of the members who might have used Mr. Moyer's repair abilities. I was drawn first of all to a father of five, complete with wife and a friendly, open face. He answered immediately and no, he hadn't used Mr. Moyer for a while as money had been tight and they were ignoring broken appliances. He did recommend him highly, however and had to leave soon for work.

There were a couple of women whose names were ticked off lightly in pencil. Perhaps I could meet them face to face at the mother/daughter banquet listed in the "Chimes" bulletin. It was Saturday, and surely I could use my influence with Robert to beat the deadline. I called, and told him not to tell Ruth, I'd make my own seating arrangements.

I didn't think she'd be too disturbed.

I promptly dropped off a mason jar at the Colonial Florist and requested an assortment of locally grown flowers, some zinnias, daisies and blue bells, to be picked up Saturday morning. "Please don't forget the lemon lilies", I added.

Saturday afternoon, Robert met me at the old fashioned dining room entrance. He looked at my flowers skeptically and led me to a table to the corner of this festively decorated room. I recognized Priscilla Potts immediately by the photo in the membership booklet, a lady somewhere in her forties, a professional blunt cut, angular face, auburn hair pulled away from the face to reveal "de rigueur" pearls. She was seated next to a friend called Grace, who introduced herself.

"Do you have room for my mother" Robert asked. "Of course we do" and a lively conversation followed about the flowers and fauna of South Jersey. Someone had a problem with aphids. "I'll look into it, I promise." I had no interest in them other than as a devious backdrop for my new mission.

Somewhere in the background a spring fashion show was occurring. Proud moms presented their brood for appraisal to the faithful members. I had to admit, it was adorable.

"You should see Prill's garden", a voice broke into my reverie of countless shows in the past, all so uplifting. Where are those cute children now? With a quick trip back to the present, "I'll be sure to, but I'm only here for one more day", I apologized, " I can stop on my way out of town." Then I ran before a refusal could begin.

That went well, I thought. I also knew I'd met a tough adversary. It would not be an easy job getting answers from this lady called Prill. Frank chose his friends well.

Robert senior and I had changed churches often on our way both up and down the social scale. I can honestly say one thing about this global group of members. The same interchangeable personalities appear over and over without fail. There's always a Grace who cheerfully accepts the roles others turn down, and so on.

This "Prill" person, however, was a woman of mystery, as yet I hadn't met her. She was a complication who might fill in some of the blanks, hopefully, I thought. I stole a quick sideways peek at her during the junior fashion show. Under straight brows, carefully shadowed eyelids of green were at half mast, cast downward as if desensitized to the present audience. A proud face, struggling to maintain its mask, so I thought.

Someone named Frank I had never met. I had been blessed.

The next day I stopped at the Potts home in an upscale neighborhood after church, (such a powerful sermon by my son, I thought. I hope the boys were as sure of themselves). As I reached the destination pointed out by my son, I went right to the back yard past the sculpted azaleas. After I checked to see Priscilla's car parked in the driveway, I gazed about thoughtfully. It had indeed been a beautiful garden, but it showed signs of neglect. "My gardener hasn't been around for a while", I heard from behind. "I'll bet", I thought to myself.

We strolled about for a bit, admiring the beautiful annuals. I could see that plans had been made, pavers had been set in place for a cozy dining area for two. It seemed as if the enthusiasm had died abruptly for the project. As Prill's soft tennis shoes disappeared into the unkempt ivy and before I excused myself, I noticed the two bottom steps of the porch. They'd been painted a pretty blue/grey and contrasted sharply with the three steps above. Their turn was obviously "next in line" for repair, a work in progress that would have to be put on hold for a while.

As I drove for home, I passed the Jerusalem Church again, but it was closed up tight.

A serene lady seemed to appear with an aura of her secrets demurely tucked under her skirts. She was silently snubbing me, daring me to invade her sanctum. Tread Carefully, Angellica!

Chapter 3

A Trip To See Clovis

The next morning Robert called me from his cell phone to praise me for my discreet behavior during the Women's spring luncheon, as if I would have behaved any other way, to my way of thinking.

"Want to take a ride today?"" he asked. ""Sure, I answered". He offered to meet me at Home Depot, where his car would be safe, and which was about half way for each of us.

He took the wheel to my relief, and we ended up in a church parking lot overlooking a field of squash. Someone had been working on the meticulous rows of yellow squash and green peppers, but it was presently empty of human life. A large green farmhouse stood to the right with a big oak tree on the side. Next to it was a smaller cottage, deserted now, and I had a good hunch as to what that might be, my son's unfortunate investment. Oh yes, nailed it!

Robert told me the whole story. It was meant for Uncle Clovis, a beloved member of the church, an elderly gentlemen who'd been helped by Mr. Moyer when his health started failing. That had been the sweetener that had sealed the deal for Robert! He, Uncle Clovis, had not lived to see his new home, regretfully.

It was time to change the subject, mostly to take his mind off Clovis. "Tell me about Priscilla Potts". I asked. "Well she's from one of the original church families way back when the church was on the boardwalk. Her father had the Ace Hardware in town, and when he passed, she stayed home and took care of her mother for years before she joined her husband. Now she works part time on the boardwalk summers making fudge. Not much else to tell", he said sadly. Well, I thought to myself, that explains the large, comfortable home that a single woman might never own.

We took a ride past Clovis' old home, down the road a bit. Instead of a "For Sale" sign there seemed to be a porch full of renters. I approached the eldest of the children and asked "When do you work on the farm"? They answered in unison, "Saturday" which was understandable. Naturally Frank had worked these newcomers into stage two of his grand plan. I mentally readjusted my weekly planner, dropped my son off at Home Depot and headed home.

Saturday found me at the farm in the empty church parking lot next door, idly reviewing this so far sparse story, until a run down blue truck appeared. I approached it and asked if I could buy some of that healthy looking squash and some peppers. The elderly gentleman said I'd have to go to the farm stand in Marlboro. I nodded as if I knew where Marlboro was and retreated quickly, before he could start thinking about any of it, and why I wasn't at the Shop Rite.

Time to get a map and find out where this as yet mythical town was!

Once home in my pretty, safe town of Sea Isle, I took another look at the Church Directory provided by Robert. A face looked out at me from all the others on the page, Dawn Nelson, with the name of the bookstore she presently owned, the Living Waters on Main Road.

The woman definitely had that young, wholesome, Swedish/Lutheran look about her, a woman who knew where she was going, and sure of how she'd get there. Those deep blue eyes were the kind of trusting ones that told of an uncomplicated life, and I made a silent prayer that she'd get there safely, with all of her resources intact, (unlike my poor son Robert). I was getting a sinking feeling about my new mission.

I had to hand it to Frank. Nice choice, Frank, a little young for you though. "When had that ever bothered men?" Never, I thought.

As for Priscilla, this man Frank Moyer also had a nose for people of substance, who'd come into their wealth by chance. What better way to pave his way through the rough patches of life? Meanwhile he fed his ego on the ones who hadn't had time to know better. Luckily there were plenty of them.

He probably had no use at all for people of his own sex who, he felt, had merely rolled over and sucked on the fruits of their lineage, with no sign of scars such as he had to tell of. It had probably never occurred to this man that there were many different kinds of "hard work"

I felt that the man was silently though sightlessly daring me to go further. Stop it, Angellica, your imagination is working overtime again. Better to put your energy toward something more useful, such as solving this paradox I'd been saddled with.

I did exactly that! I looked at the Chimes which announced a study on the book of Job to be presented shortly. I opened the book and read,"There was a man in the land of Uz whose name was Job and that man was perfect and upright and one that feared God."

L.B. Robbins

"This man was the greatest of all men in the east."

Ah, yes, perhaps there's more to tell. I welcomed the idea of something new I had never studied.

14

Chapter 4

The Bookstore

It's time for a visit to the bookstore for a Spanish/English dictionary. The Living Waters would do nicely. An elderly lady was keeping the proprietress busy so I was able to do an evaluation of this attractive intelligent blond. Glasses added to the no-nonsense visage. "Oh, no way" said my first impulse to the question of "another One?"

I have been wrong before, not often, but I'll keep my options open a while. Meanwhile, selecting a large print dictionary, I heard an "excellent choice" while the owner smiled sensibly. I had also selected a biography of Ruth, the daughter in law of the Moabite Naomi who followed her above all odds back to Judah. Not too likely to happen in the crosshairs of my life.

I'd been in need of a possible disclosure of my strange daughter–in-law's behavior for quite a while now. It was as good as any other explanation. I could indeed sympathize with my poor son who would be "stuck" once the discovery of his bad investment was discovered. It mattered not at all that her contribution was N IL.

I closed my purse, nodded to the open and friendly face behind the register and exited, heading for Sea Isle to draw my conclusions in the privacy of my home. No, I'll take a small detour to a small farm market on my way home, time to stock up on more squash and peppers (Thank you GPS, another gift included in the purchase of my car).

There it was ahead "Elliot's Home Grown". I selected some blueberries and peaches which I actually wanted and pursued the green and yellow squash, keeping an eye out for the most loose lipped of the employees. Yes, he was headed my way, making friendly comments along the way.

"These must be Mr. Moyer's" as I approached him upon entering my sphere. "Oh yes, Maam, No chemicals - he uses no chemicals." "This is my freezing season", I added impulsively. "I'm interested in negotiating a deal with him, and I've missed him in church, when can I see him"? He responded in kind to my (recently acquired) graying granny knot with "Well, he delivers Saturdays or you can just go up to Addisons".

I thanked him and left quickly in my lucky Town Car. It left some people with the impression that I had done something successfully. Oh, well! I headed out to the little post office I had noticed in this quaint farming town.

As I arrived home, I carried in my latest produce purchases, placed them in the kitchen and created a fruit salad. I fed my hungry cats and kittens, and then settled down to watch the evening news.

I loved the evening news. My mind always jumped ahead from the seemingly innocent news to the more evil plot behind, performed by some distant, unsuspected third party. There was no mention of a Frank Moyer, missing lately from the Atlantic county area.

I reviewed the Directory my son Robert had provided to aid me in my search. Under the name of Moyer, true to form, were no pictures, no wife, only the mention of a son named

Scott, who was in college somewhere out in the West, (or so I'd heard). Then I glanced again at the "Chimes" bulletin I read that the study of the Book of Job Wednesday evening, would be lead by Earl Davis, whom I had discarded as a useful candidate. Still, he had a warm sense of humor. I needed that right now.

Next I called Robert to tell him that I would be attending the study of Job on Wednesday evening. I would be dropping off a meatless casserole before class and might have some good news for him.

For now, I had better read ahead in the book of Job to get a jump on the class.

I moved to the parlor and sat down in Rob's comfortable chaise. I read, Job was told "Thy sons and thy daughters were eating and drinking in their elder brother's home. And behold a great wind there came from the wilderness and smote the four corners of the house and it fell upon the young men and they are all dead." And Job spoke, "Naked came I out of my mother's womb and naked shall I return thither. The Lork gave and the Lord taketh away, blest be the name of the Lord".

I must have nodded off, for the stubborn click of the timer announced it was time to shift position upstairs for bed. I was not in the Land of Ur as I thought but in Sea Ilse City, where someone named Priscilla Potts had need of my help.

I though again of the address I'd gotten from the white pages of the little Marlboro post office, the only rural route delivery box for Addison. Perhaps my mission was accomplished and I'd be no longer needed. That, unfortunately was not to be true. Those old farmers seemed to have their own secret network that went back over the centuries.

I now knew the "where" of the elusive Frank Moyer but was still not at all sure of the "why". Happily, however that was not part of my assigned mission.

As I thought of Priscilla, what bothered me still were those sad, sad eyes of of hers as she sighed toward her unfinished garden and perhaps her unfinished life. Her hair was graying faster than mine, though mine was cosmetic. The pain in her eyes seemed to cut deep down into her soul and somehow I'd like to know the cause of that pain.

Moreover, speaking of the cause of her pain, where was he anyway with my son's money, and more to the point, why was he not in his own home?

Tomorrow's problem, I thought.

Chapter 5

A Trip to Farm Country

The next morning I answered the phone in my robe. It was Robert, more upset if possible, than our luncheon meeting at Docks. After my phone call to him about my newfound address, he'd deciphered the code from the RR code (with the help of an old timer from the church). He wanted to take a ride out to the Addisons. Over coffee I explained my reluctance to accompany him unless he made a promise to remain in the car, as we were dealing with a criminal mindset. I did realize that there was no stopping him, I'd better go if only to deflect trouble. He was visibly upset and I couldn't exactly blame him, but this was not the time for irrational tantrums. Time instead for mature appearances and an agreeable smile. Trust me, Robert.

Years ago I could always hold out the promise of a trip to the zoo. That time was gone, and long ago. He promised resolutely to do the grown up thing and to stay in the car while we were there. He would need some time while he drove to make a plan and so would I.

The neighborhood became more rural as time passed. I had forgotten how pretty South Jersey could be in springtime. My mind was back in my beloved Bucks County and I almost saw

Amish carriages and covered bridges with those darling pink cheeked, braided, children. "Why did I not bring a camera?" I said as he suddenly swung left into a long lane with a tired sign at the entrance. There were, as expected, neat rows of pepper and squash to greet us as we passed.

"Looks like we've hit pay dirt" I said aloud. There were no signs of life anywhere, just an old farmhouse with faded and broken gingerbread above the spacious porch, an elegant one in its day. The inevitable forget-me-nots were stubborn proof of that era.

Despite my protests, Robert jumped out of the car with me and got to the doorbell first. An elderly lady appeared at the sight of our ring with white hair and delicate, transparent skin. Her sad eyes looked to the east, and seemed to say "I will lift up mine eyes to the the hills", but instead landed back on earth with "Can I help you dear"?

I answered with "we've been planning a new senior center in town and we thought you'd like to take part in the meetings". Robert looked as if he'd never met me before and was ready to deny the whole trip with this crazy, out of touch, lady. My eyes challenged him with "come on Robert, do you want to solve this or not!"

"Not at this time, dear, my Edward is in the hospital and no one is sure what will happen.

Maybe another time," was her sorrowful reply.

"I'm sorry, if you need our help, please call" and I extended a written name and phone number for this sweet lady to call. "I mean it?", and I sincerely did, as a scary thought passed over me as fleeting as the winged flight of the eagle above.

"I have help. My cousin's nephew is here to help out. Edward insisted on it."

Before we left I noticed a sign of recent construction on the antiquated garage door trim.

It was painted blue/grey. No surprise at all. This Frank Moyer seemed to make tracks around south Jersey, but why? Why would so sensible a farmer as this, so careful to tend his plants and take care of his chores, leave a comfortable farmhouse such as his, and bury himself in a forgotten farming town? The puzzle was far from being solved, and there were too few clues to this strange mystery.

It was time to go home and look at this ever increasingly complex story with a new set of eyes.

Early in the evening I was relieved to be at home again, sitting on my back porch where everything made sense. I was alone with Chloe and her new kittens. All three were white with grey caps on their heads. Chloe was no longer just an other stray using my porch to birth her babies, she was a positive sign that life goes on, no matter what perversion was taking place.

My mind was reviewing this puzzling new side of Frank Moyer, caring, yet with too much acquisitiveness.

What a chilling thought; someone you had included in your family circle, someone you'd trusted completely had penetrated this cloud of comfort you called home.

What do we know about this bird of prey?

He circles endlessly, seeking a chink in your armor.

He can be ready in a second to turn your assets into a buffet lunch once he's isolated them.

Finally, he will always be selecting new recruits as victims in his plan, perhaps a man of the cloth, who wouldn't understand revenge and might not look for appearances of evil within his family circle.

God said it better than I ever could in the Book of Job in reply to His question to Satan of where he had been. "going to and fro in the earth walking up and down in it….seeking whom I may to devour.

Well and good, Angellica, but how does this move the investigation forward?

Let's try another tack.

I visited my daily planner and inserted a note to revisit the Living Waters Bookstore in bold print. Dawn Nelson seemed to be an element of youth and vitality in complete contrast to the lethal character of this complex web!

Talk to me Dawn.

Chapter 6

The Bible Study

Wednesday around dinner time I pulled into the long tree lined drive way, around to the back of the Lutheran parsonage. I pulled my town car up to the quaint old Victorian porch, the finest aspect of this stately old home, to be greeted by "Yeah, it's Nana, Mom". My son came out of his victory garden, took hold of my picnic basket and overnight case, and put them in their respective places. I set the table cloth and the meatless casserole on the table, along with the video game for the boys, perhaps they wouldn't need college after all.

As the twins headed toward their computer, Robert surprised me with a sheepish grin and "remember you asked what I might have done to Frank to anger him to take this kind of revenge, it might have been this. In our last meeting before our vacation, I announced that the consistory had decided to drop our support for the college scholarship fund. It was a slam dunk to go to Frank's son Scott, a natural straight "A" student, way out in front of the pack. Still, not fair to the others."

I looked at the dejected slope of his shoulders, and passed at the chance to say "I wish we would have discussed this six months ago" and instead said "Like it or not son, there's your answer. You damaged his ego and struck financially at the same time."

"Well, he retorted, no one but Frank benefited, and we sure could use the money better." About that time the iced tea appeared and we abruptly ended our conversation. I now had the "why" to the puzzle at hand solved. .

During dinner, we discussed the weather, the traffic and the lack of rain. My son retrieved his Bible, notes and we headed out to the Bethlehem Lutheran Church. It was a grand Swedish style columned building. The story went that the sixty or so members had sold their building on the boardwalk to a casino, and now they had to grow their membership to fit their new building. My poor son had his hands full, he really didn't need this problem that was being dumped on him. Everyone had gotten into the gambling spirit. Now they were gambling on my son Robert.

We parked in the 'clergy only' spot and headed inside. Our little study group was seated at the back of this beautiful marble and oak sanctuary. While Robert headed back to the meeting with his trustees, I made a silent prayer for guidance in my new mission.

"Man that is born of a woman is of few days and full of trouble," our leader began with. I could quite agree wholeheartedly, and I was prepared to learn with an open mind. Job certainly understood trials better than anyone else in his neck of the woods ever could have. I'd better pay attention.

After we prayed and had a lively discussion of Job, we were officially dismissed and I headed over to Priscilla's friend Grace. Although I had prepared an introduction, I had no need to do so, she was so open and easy to talk to. Grace was one of those rare individuals who knew her mind and her age, and had no problem with either.

"I wish I had gotten to know Clovis ", I sadly responded, when she told me she missed his ready mind in these meetings.

"You know, his death came upon all of us, so suddenly, we didn't get a chance to visit and bring meals over, as we always do with those who are feeling down. I'm not at all sure that any of us know what was wrong with him. Frank assured us that all he needed was a little rest and he'd be back to his old self."

I cleverly switched the topic to Priscilla Potts and her lovely garden.

"Something is just 'not right' with Prill, she sighed as she reflected on her close friend.

She felt she (Prill) had something bothering her that she just needed to talk about. She was distracted, disinterested in friends and appearance. "Not like Prill at all" as she hung her head sadly.

I asked if she thought Prill might welcome some company or words of comfort from a friend from the church family.

"Oh. She'll let you know for sure!"

As Robert and I returned home, I told him of my talk with Grace. "Don't give up", I lied.

"I feel like we're really getting close"

We headed home, each to his own room and his own thoughts. When I'd pressed Robert about his meeting with the Trustees, it seemed no one at all was surprised at Frank's "no show". He was simply being himself in his own secretive way.

Once inside the tiny manse guest room, I eagerly collapsed into the bed that had been purchased for Robert in his teens , along with his dresser. My thoughts were clearly all around and above the bed we had so carefully planned for our son's. success (in whatever venture life had in store).

"Ah, Mr. Moyer, sir, my son unwittingly found the soft spot in your armor which protected that tough ego of yours. You had planned to profit from a life of leisure that only college could provide for your son, Scott, at the expense of the Lutheran church.

You must have silently dreamt of that since he was a child, and now the fantasy might be drawing to a close."

What a chilling revenge on a person not known to you at all for thwarted that dream.

You were the recipient of quick cunning, which could project you into a lucrative mortgage at six percent, knowing full well that you could only provide payment for two weeks or so. If the plan worked, you wouldn't have to, since you luckily possessed the only copy of that mortgage

You must have been a trapper in your teens. Yes, the lure, the enticement with just the perfect bait that each creature needed, just before letting the trap door down for the kill.

With that I sighed and entered the world of the twilight zone.

"Acquaint now thyself with Him and be at peace."

I

Chapter 7

More Complications

It was early evening. As I lounged on my back porch to share my thoughts with my new kittens, three adorable new citizens of earth, I reviewed my present success or non-success of the day.

It was always here on this porch that I was always able to put myself in a better mood, a different, happier mood or a deeper, sharper or more clever state of mind depending on the need. This was the only area in our new home that Rob and I had planned together, in one of his bouts of remission of this terrible disease, this cancer who knew no mercy toward his victims, this cheater of the game of life.

As I relaxed in one of our matching chairs, I could picture Rob, as he worked on his charged up laptop, humming softly, "The queen was in the parlor ---", as he scrutinized the various entities of our small portfolio. Why hadn't I shown some interest or asked some questions of his sharp mind? Then, of course, he would always be there, wouldn't he? It might be time to put the laptop to some other use. Where was is anyway?

I felt I was working all around the edges of the case, but something was missing, and I couldn't quite put my hands on it. Something quite near yet far was escaping me. One of the four people hadn't trusted him completely. It was Dawn Nelson. She had never joined the swelling crowd of admirers.

Once again, I had to send out feelers, get her to say something unexpected, break her out of her silence. (It was strange, Frank's gravitation to quite people, no not strange.) Better make plans to visit the bookstore to scare up more background on our favorite lady killer. I hated doing this, I'd promised Robert to proceed alone to uncover the mystery of what was going on in this man's life, but it was quite impossible.

We'd discovered where he was living, but not much more. We had no idea what kind of pressure could be brought on him to restore the money he had pilfered. He was not a criminal by nature or historically, he was a loyal trustee. So what was going on? I needed a breakthrough to see behind that thick skull that was Frank Moyer, some insignificant clue to his present crisis that might bring this mystery home.

I did just that, I revisited the bookstore. Oddly the porch was painted blue/grey.

Once inside my eyes were drawn to the drawn to the delightful Noah's Ark nook, very artistic, this nook, presided over by a comforting giraffe. He'd probably entertained many a "Horton Hears A Who" audiences, along with the wise parrot on his shoulder.

The present owner was quite gifted, I thought

Dawn was her pretty, fresh self as she faced another new day in a stylish canvas frock that I didn't quite recognize. "We have to talk. I'm Pastor Peterson's mother and I need your help. You seem like someone who can be trusted to be discreet." It seemed I'd removed the veil that had been covering the cheerful mask that had been Dawn Nelson. Bleak sadness appeared in its place.

New that she'd let her guard down she reluctantly agreed to meet with me while she closed for lunch. That struck me as strange. The bookstore was across the street from a lovely park- a good place to meet on a beautiful spring day. A deli nearby provided sandwiches and the setting was complete with the newly budding cherry trees.

"It's about Frank Moyer" I broke out with. "How did you know?" she jumped in. Think fast Angellica, there's more to this story, a whole lot more. "They'd never divorced, so how could I know he was still married, and if I suspected it, I somehow hoped he'd fall in love with me and do the right thing," she said sadly.

I wanted to know more, to control the conversation, but I knew better than to break the spell Dawn had fallen into. Tell me how it started", I broke in having decided to build on the momentum of truth I was the lucky beneficiary of. The tuna sandwiches would have to wait.

"We met at a Bible study at the home of one of the members. It seemed innocent enough. He had that "hurting look" of the newly separated and found out along the way that I was looking for a small bookshop. I had a small divorce settlement which I had to be careful with. He said he'd had a lot of experience with sheriff sales and he'd help. Well, he was a great help and we became close friends, or so I thought."

She hung her head in shame about the relationship that had somehow morphed into something she hadn't expected, and told me she was ending it.

First of all, it seamed to be going nowhere. She'd had a happy marriage at one time and recognized emptiness instead of happiness, all too well. No meeting with friends, no making plans that would be fun for the future, all the excitement was missing, like a marriage that was already failing. There were quick dinners in a very small kitchen, instead of checking out one of the many new cafes that were opening in town, like so many happy young couples in love seemed to do. In short, it was more like an affair with a married man. He didn't even attend Sunday morning church services as he had to do his farm work.

Ah. The confidence of youth! In short he had less time on his hand than she had.

Dawn continued. "I did seem to notice that he never spoke of himself or shared intimate thoughts. I also noticed that my drab little kitchen was picking up a cheerful new appearance, new stove, restored cabinets. In short I was happy here, enjoying impromptu meals, prepared with surprise ingredients that accompanied his visits.

He always left as quickly as he arrived without promises or mention of his next visit. If he ever called again, she planned to call it off. Happily, he seemed to sense this and hadn't called. Another possibility, his present difficulties were taking up a whole lot more time than he could afford.

Wow, I thought, you asked for it, you got it! Now, what to do with this new information?

"Dawn, do you think he'll call again", I was merely stretching out my time for this visit, I know, but I had to press on for Robert's sake. Time was getting short.

"Oh, you can be sure of that", she answered, "Twice, any way. Then I'll be finished with my payments to him". She seemed to be understanding the true Frank Moyer as the real world saw him, or at any rate, as I saw him.

At the sheriff's sale, as Dawn explained she'd picked a perfect little shop, by location. It was the only one close to the boardwalk. She, however, was short of the ten percent cash that was required to close the deal at the auction.

Frank excused himself and ran out to his truck, returning with the balance.

The seduction was complete!

Chapter 8

Priscilla Potts

I awoke early the next morning. I suddenly wanted to deal with The Truth as I knew it. Why shouldn't this surprise me? So many lies and deceptions seemed to totally surround me. It was beginning to get me down, as none of these lies were of my own making. (I could deal with them otherwise.)

"Priscilla," as I lifted the phone, "I'm in the neighborhood and I've got to see you. I'll be there shortly," as I quickly hung up before she could think of an excuse. I was sure Frank Moyer was one of the sources of the crazy maze she had wrapped herself in. I had no idea why, but I knew that if she could only enlighten me as to the source of her sadness, I might be able to help her. In fact I was sure I could do so. She was lucky to have such a friend as Grace, who'd only said "there's no fool like an old fool". Yes, that phrase clinched it, explaining the unfortunate condition of the whole history of aging womankind.

As she carefully opened the door to my knock, crushed eyes and unkempt hair met my unwelcome visit. I burst inside, contrary to my normally quiet and shy nature. "It's about your gardener, I know where he is and I'm sorry I've not been more honest with you". I shoved some blueberry muffins into her hands and explained my intrusion into her privacy with a

"Here, peace offering, please let me explain but there's more money missing from another source."(Sorry Robert. I'd tried other avenues and they didn't work).

"I already know, we've spoken on his cell phone. I'll be right with you", as she headed to the kitchen with her new stash to decide, I think, in the privacy of her kitchen how much to tell me. "I'm glad you came, I needed to talk to somebody". I'd guessed correctly, a life of secrecy was not what she was accustomed to, thankfully she trusted me.

I spent the time admiring the surrounding which I found myself in. The well appointed chair rail, moldings, fireplace and tasteful furniture told of a life carefully lead accompanied by a comfortable income. A grandfather clock softly chimed "We're doing quite well here, thank you."

She returned with an assortment of pastries and some coffee and nervously whispered "Please explain why you have to know where he is". She settled uncomfortably in her white linen love seat.

"Your friend Gracie told me a little about the bad business deal you'd made. You weren't the only one, and it's even worse." Priscilla looked at me as if she had been expecting this all along.

There's another women in the picture who's been wronged. It's Dawn Nelson." I simply placed my words on a different emphasis as I rearranged the facts. "Angellica" (to myself) "adding more deception to an already confusing story is not quite the Christian alternative", but then when has life ever been simple?

Priscilla looked at me warily above her coffee mug. "Your right, there's more to this story". Then she surprised me, soulfully, with "Frank, why did you have to do it?"

A tear dropped silently.

She and I seemed to have come to some kind of unspoken agreement.

"Frank came to the Addison's at first for purely unselfish reasons at first. Mr. Addison had been diagnosed with a fatal viral infection and was not expected to live. They had no children and Edward was concerned about his wife's health and safety. They asked Frank, his nephew, to stay with her until her nerves improved.

Shortly after being there, Frank called her (Prill), and asked her to meet him at the truck stop on route 95. She arrived and nearly did not recognize the handsome face which met her, he hadn't shaved, very unusual for him, and was frightened. "Having a meltdown", he said.

"Ed is fully recovered and he's coming home Saturday" he said. "Why Frank, that's wonderful" she'd stated. "No it certainly is not!"

He continued with his narrative. "Uncle Ed told me to take care of his wife in any way possible, and he gave me the combination to his safe to do it with. I was doing real well until the letter came from the college stating the final tuition was due for Scott".

"Carlie always felt that Scott didn't belong with the upper classes in an Ivy League school, and I should have listened. I might have done a few things wrong, but I got the tuition taken care of."

I few things wrong, I thought. This man needed a lesson in ethics. The temptation was too great for Frank, the rest was history.

He seemed better already and said he'd be in touch. We both knew why!

I let myself out. Priscilla seemed not to notice, rather she seemed to have aged considerably over this last hour of chilling truth..

It seemed Frank Moyer's son was not in the west somewhere, but was in Cambridge, that privileged place where the wealthy secretly met to iron out the details of their future personal lives. Rob and I had taken a bus tour of the town one summer. Harvard University, the Holy Grail of the smart set, the Fogg Museum and the commons were not home to anyone we knew, but it was the place where Scott Moyer had selected as his neighborhood, or rather his father had.

No wonder few in the church knew about it!

I now knew that Frank Moyer didn't waste his time with people he couldn't scam money off of. Those loyal farmers Frank knew so well were completely safe from his raw greed. There was just nothing left of their wealth to separate them from. What Prill had invested in was of no interest to me, I only know it existed.

I also knew why most of the Moyer family had left the church, embarrassment.

Yes, this Back Neck family knew that this blue chip community of Cambridge was not where many of them dropped their shoes and called home. At least few of them made it there, and few made it there honestly!

Chapter 9

The Phone Call

I had barely returned to my home in Sea Isle City, when the phone rang urgently. It was Priscilla Potts and she was quite unnerved. "Thank Heavens, you answered. Something awful has happened. My life has become a nightmare"

"Please sit down, Prill" I felt I could use the friendly diminutive that Grace used, I felt a newfound closeness to her, after her recent confidences to me. "Breathe slowly, and tell me what happened", I urged. This poor woman who asked nothing of anyone, who had been so hurt, for no reason of her own making.

"I've just had a visit from Carlie, Frank's wife, or ex-wife as I had thought. I had decided to help him out. I was thinking how quickly he'd always responded to my calls for help, he had never refused, he came right over. Carlie pulled up and stormed into my home. I'm not sure how she even knew where I lived. She'd been following him it seemed."

"Incredibly, she wants to get back with him. She said they'd never really divorced when she left him, she'd always assumed they'd get back together. Lately they'd begun to try dating again, not officially, but they met at her apartment, dined and spent the evening together, just like in the old days." It seemed that absence had made the heart grow fonder, as the saying justly went, I thought. Now her landlord was selling the apartment. When she suggested she move back in with him again, he violently opposed the thought. According to Frank, they'd never gotten along as well as now. They no longer lived together and there were no more arguments about money or their son's expensive education.

He reminded her of her violent temper

Prill continued, "Carlie was visibly upset and I began to fear for my safety, she was a large woman and quite out of control." Then she added. "When I asked her what she would do she rushed out and said 'You'll see, you'll all see'".

'Prill, you've got to get out of there at once". She knew it and was already packing to spend the night with Grace, where she was always welcome and she knew it.

At this point, Frank's deception was complete. Prill had been expecting this, but the extent of this brash lie was unthinkable. A large clump of fear and doubt fell to the back of her throat and down onto the background of her mind.

I didn't sleep well at all that night. I was truly perplexed. This story was developing too many canals that didn't quite flow together at all, too many paths for my simple life, and getting worse. The source of the mystery, Frank Moyer, seemed driven at first by old fashioned virtues of church, hard work and small time village. Now, he seemed to have three women in his life, and serious relationships with all of them. Did he care-truly care for any of them, maybe none of them.

It was hard to tell!

I might as well get out of bed, review the facts of the phone call and write down the story as I saw it, in my little planner, within the confines of my comfortable bedroom. I glanced over at the empty side of the four poster, and yes, it was still as empty as it was the night before.

Carlie, Frank's long forgotten wife, had used the opportunity earlier in the evening, to share some of her husband's preferred life styles.

"He always liked his girls to be living alone in single houses, so he could visit whenever he wanted to and not be seen by neighbors."

I added to myself, "and going home alone to an empty house could only complete this dream come true lifestyle."

"Darn it, Frank, you ought to know by now that this was getting too complicated and rarely works!" Now, more than likely he'd never return home and, worse yet I might never get to meet this South Jersey Romeo, this small bit actor who was setting breaking hearts all over Atlantic county! I stood very little chance of recovering what was Robert's, moreover.

All at once I knew why Frank had been so eager to escape from his home and find refuge with distant relatives If only greed hadn't overtaken him, he'd be safe for now in his secret little compound, safe from this emotional tempest that was brewing.

I headed out the next morning for Grace's after getting directions for her home. I was so worried about Prill. After coffee however, we managed to add some humor and even made her laugh a little.

I thought I was so special," Prill was saying over a delicious cheese omelet, flavored with fresh herbs "I even thought those Thursday evenings were unique in my specially designed 'Kitchen by Frank'!" He seemed so happy and content working on my new indoor charcoal grill- I'd buy Kobe steaks or lamb chops and he'd grill them to perfection. I thought life couldn't get any better than this".

"Now I realize that when I took that vacation for two weeks in New Orleans, that celibacy was a human condition he never cared for."

"Well, cheer up, Grace said, there's only seven days in the week. He's bound to taper off!" At least we'd left her laughing!

As she walked me out to my car, Grace confided that she could have spared her friend a little grief by sharing what Frank's sister, Luda, had told her before she slipped off of the membership roles at church. She felt that her brother possessed little ability to draw others to the gospel while he felt himself exempt from the constraints put upon followers of the Lord to adhere to, particularly the married ones. That those biblical precepts were meant for people with less ability than he was obvious! She hadn't known him for a lifetime for nothing, it seemed.

To myself, I thought as I started the long trek home to Sea Isle, his other alternative Dawn had started to see her hero in a new light. The process of peeling away the protective layers of his shallow disregard for women had let a new coldness into the relationship. Time for a new port in a storm, Frank, or perhaps an older more comfortable port!

Well and good for now. Next for the hard part, telling Robert about the "new Babylonia" that was festering among the communicants at the Bethlehem Lutheran Church, I only hoped this wasn't the tip of the glacier. I had no magic remedy for this new wrinkle, either. I don't think anyone ever has.

Poor Prill, my heart ached for her. All the clues were there, she just didn't recognize them. Love is strange.

Chapter 10

Back in My Kitchen

I needn't have worried at all about contacting my son Robert. He was pounding on my door at 10:00 the next morning. His cowlick stood at right angles to his head. Not good!

"I don't know if you've heard or not. I can't imagine you have! It's about Frank Moyer's wife. Everyone at the church is talking about it. She rammed into the front of their home with an SUV yesterday, just drove up the lane and into the house with the van three times, went into the house and walked back down the lane. Some farm workers next door told someone about it through an interpreter."

"The deacons got some men to back the SUV out of the house, and secured the opening. They feel it's the least they can do, they couldn't get in touch with him. He's been a good friend for a long time."

I had settled Robert down in my kitchen, and did what good mothers do, fixed bacon and eggs with bacon gravy (my mid west background kicked in). It felt good to be a "Mom" again and really needed.

While Robert rambled on about what seemed to me totally predictable, I was comparing my kitchen to that of Priscilla Potts. I had snuck a peek on the way out.. The marble countertops, tiled floors, stainless appliances, and especially the island with indoor/outdoor pit, set off by French doors, why the man was pure genius. Let's face it, a few minor indiscretions maybe, but he was definitely a keeper.

"What was I saying" I rebuked myself. I was falling in line with his other conquests and suddenly I was in touch with Frank's lethal allure to otherwise sensible women. I had truly felt that I would have been immune, but oh no, not so! A lesson learned, learned well indeed..

Priscilla had confided in me that she's never been happier than on those Thursday evenings when they'd prepared dinner in the new kitchen created just for her. Now I might never get to meet him face to face. There was no reason for Frank to return home now! He didn't seem to be the type who could face the consequences of his own actions.

My thoughts were interrupted by "Do you have any of that cranberry jelly you always make?" Oh my, I thought, how many years ago was that? "I'll make some". Sure, I thought, that might make a plan.

Over coffee on the back porch, as we settled into my matching chairs I told him of the events and of his (Frank's) many women. Most especially of what had made Carlie Moyer angry.

"I guess you won't be attending bible study this evening. They do really like you, you know." He seemed bewildered by this fact. No, I thought, I wouldn't miss it for the world.

I thought Robert's reaction to this rather tempestuous story was strangely lackluster.

Perhaps, I mused, that was why he sought comfort in neutral, passionless women such as Ruth.

Before I left for the class on the book of Job, I received a call from Grace to tell me she would pass on the class for the evening, and instead would be seeing a movie with Prill instead. Surely one of the 12 movies being viewed would be interesting. I doubted it, but gave cheerful encouragement anyway.

Grace was not only a good friend, (unlike Job's) but was a true student of the Word . She was passing up the chance to be a true celebrity with insider information. She also knew how easy it would be to slip pieces of gossip delightfully and unintentionally into an eager crowd. I was impressed. I stuck to the weather, traffic and the book of Job...

"Where wast thou when I laid the foundations of the earth." This came out of the whirlwind from our recent study and yes, Job, I thank you for your eloquence and wisdom.

If this class could have molded such personalities as Grace and her friend Prill, then this was truly a worthy goal to aim for. I would revisit the book of Job.

In the privacy of my home, my thoughts went back to this "restless evil" that this ongoing mystery was becoming. Something told me more was to follow, and it wouldn't be good news for anyone.

No, not good at all!

Chapter 11

The Shocking Truth

However much of an eerie feeling of unease about the preceding events I'd had, I was no way prepared for the actual horror to follow. Frank Moyer had been shot!

This is what happened ---as I was able to piece together from the telephone conversations of both Prill and my son Robert. Someone who must have been privy to Frank's cell number had notified him as to the damage to his home. It hadn't been Prill, she'd assured me, she was just too unsure of her feelings to speak to him, and more than a little bit annoyed with his dishonestly. All of his ability for repair, and his endless tools to do just this with, he'd returned in his truck to take care of this task. No surprise to anyone who knew him.

Apparently, while on the ladder nailing boards to the frame, he must have turned to see who was calling to him, and was shot in the back. His partner came on the scene shortly

as he had received a call from Frank to meet him there, luckily for him. His partner could not be the one who'd called Frank (he'd made the call to 911). Whoever had called must have been lying in wait, someone who knew he'd be there immediately. Frank was barely alive and was 'medi vac'd to Cooper Hospital south of Philly. A lot of prayer had gone out for him, and only God the author of life and death, knew his future.

A call of outrage had gone out for his wife!

Just an hour earlier, after my call from Prill, I was reflecting that her last words to me had been "You know, Carlie just loved him too much to do this. I never really felt threatened by her, I only felt sympathy." Kind Prill, she was incapable of understanding evil in her rosy colored world. She said goodby, she had to hurry, she was on her way to Philly to see Frank.

My minds eye could see again that short winding road up the hill to the little church where Robert and I had parked and the small farm with its green farmhouse and the as yet precariously owned cottage of my son. The image was so picturesque you could see Peter rabbit burrowing under the log railing and munching on a carrot. A sniper shooting at its hard working owner, no never! Unthinkable at least.

In the evening, Action News at 12 came on the TV. Speaking of Frank Moyer, my short prophesy had been fulfilled. They were at Atlantic City Airport, announcing that Frank Moyer of Pleasantville had been shot by an "as yet unknown assailant" and was recovering at Cooper Hospital. His son was shown on camera exiting from his flight at Atlantic City Airport, having just heard the bad news about his father. His eyes were facing the ground and the media left him alone to grieve. Not a homecoming anyone would have wished for, and after so much time away at school.

I needed to talk to the third person of interest again, who seemed to be in the center of this storm called "Frank Moyer". I knew Dawn still had strong feelings for Frank. She was as yet unaware of his busy alternative lives. Tomorrow I'd go once again to the Living Waters Bookstore.

Chapter 12

Living Waters

"Dawn, my dear child, I'm so sorry" I said as I entered the little shop. "Oh, Angellica, I can't tell you how bad I feel. How could I say those awful things about Frank after all he's done for me"..

We were alone. I had deliberately gone very early in the morning. "We were friends, more than anything else, and this never should have happened. He's such a good person.

Who could have done this awful thing? As far as Frank was concerned, he really didn't have any hatred, or any feelings at all about his wife. I don't believe she did it. He repaired anything she needed fixed. Why would anyone hurt someone who did this?" Dear Dawn was so practical.

I guided her gently over to a bench beneath the wise giraffe and comforted her there. It had all been a dream, not built upon a solid foundation at all, but upon what was most plentiful around here, sand. It was a sandcastle created for a child, and, like Frank's life, about as fragile.

I must keep a close eye on her, I thought, as I looked up to her friendly family of jungle animals, and made a promise to them to restore the childhood of her not too distant past.

This adult life, full of its snares and traps was not one to be lightly entered into without the proper weapons. I'll help you find them, I silently pledged.

"Well," I said, "I just came to offer my sympathies to you, I'm sure not many members would realize they were in order. You're two very private people, and I can respect that, but the woman in me knew you would be hurting. It was such a violent act, it just doesn't make sense at all".

Dawn was crying very softly now. I knew she needed to do that. "I was so angry with him, just because he wasn't joining my little parade and conforming with what would be normally expected. I've always been a little stubborn, headstrong even. It probably ruined my first marriage, but no one ever said that Frank was normal," (no, not normal at all, I thought)", and I didn't recognize that. It probably added to his appeal."

That, I thought, was an understatement. Please don't enter into any more complicated relationships, Dawn.

"Don't get down on yourself, dear."

"Men are just more complicated than we give them credit for, and, the thought of another marriage so soon after an unhappy one can put real fear into the bravest of them all".

We laughed, which was my intention after all, but what followed I was not prepared for.

Once again Dawn had given me the unexpected. "Just look on the bright side, Dawn. You probably might not have to make the final payments" I said, purely in jest.

"Oh no." she said. The serious Dawn was back in the present. "The deed on my shop was prepared by the sheriff's department. It is not in Frank's name. He put his son's name on it, so his wife couldn't touch it I assume. I really didn't care at the time." She trusted Frank, that was for sure, and she said that Scott was incapable of making a move without his father's blessing.

This case continued to get more complicated all the time, I said to myself as I headed home. Dawn, true to her nature, had a real passion for books, children's books mostly, but no real passion for the law.

For the present, I'd have to have a talk with Robert. For some reason this talk with Dawn had put me in mind of my son, who also had such high hopes for mankind.

I had found a new admiration for Frank. One thing about him was certain. Had Frank Moyer aimed for a man on a ladder with a loaded shotgun, the outcome would have been fixed, there would be no lingering coma at all!

Oh no, that steady hand that never missed a nail would surely have targeted and not missed a vital organ. These South Jersey grunts rarely miss their targets.

Chapter 13

A Killer on the Loose

My worst fears were realized. Frank Moyer had lost the battle for his life at 3:00 in the morning. We were all stunned. I personally had always believed his life was charmed, it seemed to be at least, and I wasn't prepared for the emptiness I felt. I had believed him to be larger than life, a man for all seasons, or perhaps a "man for all ages".

It wasn't like me to be frozen in inactivity. I was always the "energizer", never at a loss for enthusiasm, but I that knew someone I liked would be going to jail for murder. I forced myself to put on a pot of coffee, and hoped this wildly unexpected news would project me into some sort of activity.

Robert was at the door. He explained that he had just left an elder's meeting and headed for the closest chair. He sunk into it, putting his head in his hands and said exhaustedly, "You know, Mom, it wasn't Carlie at all. She has an ironclad alibi". It seemed the doctor she'd been working for had noticed her erratic behavior and suggested it might be chemical or even worse. His office had helped to arranged testing at the University of Penn for her and set it up for the week of her vacation, despite her protests. She had told no one about it, and was in fact in denial, but was meekly accompanied by staff to her appointment, that very day in question…

"Well", I thought with relief, "it was just like this wild story to have no logical ending. We ended our brief conversation, and Robert left, as quickly as he arrived. No point in saying anything more. I just wanted to be alone and crash. Perhaps some answer could be provided from above, I was flat out of solutions.

I went to bed early that evening. "Lord, if you want to use me, so be it, but please return me to the uncomplicated life I 'm far more used to. Thy will be done".

I dreamt of an endless sea of boats, way offshore, all tossing to and 'fro with no pattern, but the uncertain trade winds of Sea Isle City. Worst of all, I had promised to bake a cake for the memorial service. Oh, no, why had I done that?

As the sun came through my bedroom blinds, I awoke surprisingly refreshed. What was it I'd meant to ask Robert about his mortgage. I couldn't place it. There was a killer at large and that was all I was sure of!

I'd fed the cats, put on the coffee and came back to life as I knew it. The story was on the local morning news, repetitions of what I already knew. Now, there it was, the word "killer at large being sought by the police, If any one knew"…etc.

Life went on, plans were being made for a large service, or one was expected at any rate.

The Moyers were a large family, or so I'd heard. The killer was thought to be an unknown burglar, by everyone but me, who knew better.

Chapter 14

The Service

Robert's small congregation did what churches do best, consoling the grief stricken. They united enthusiastically to give a beautiful memorial to Frank Moyer, perhaps because they had so easily and erroneously accepted his wife as the shooter. This gesture was for her, their way of asking forgiveness. As the organ softly played, the solemn mood was felt all around.

Grace, Prill and I were riding shotgun for his wife, ready to give aquick escort to the door to anyone who mentioned the couple's separation, or who doubted her right to legitimately grieve There was happily no need to do so. Everyone simply expressed their sorrow and offers of help should there be a need, as Frank had always been the first to do so. There was no doubt anywhere, his presence would be sorely missed.

I was so proud of Robert. His short message was from the Book of James, "Every good and perfect gift is from above." Frank's gift had been the gift of "helps" and he was always the first to be there with his truck full of tools. He reminded us that Frank's last trip had been to help a distant relative in time of need, and he hadn't advertised it, as was his nature, he just "showed up" when needed. Some members stood up and added testimonial to that fact, with personal stories. One elderly lady said, with tears in her eyes, she just couldn't see where she could go for help now.

As I looked around, I noted two things. Dawn Nelson was seated quietly in the back row, mourning alone in simple homespun grey and bravely holding up her home front. She now had the assurance that her first impression had been correct all along. He was a married man. Another dream washed away with the tide. Also, Scott Moyer was not in attendance. This was not the time to ask why not, we would find out when the time was right to do so.

I joined the line waiting to pay respects to the casket in the front of the chapel, surrounded by flowers upon flowers, a solemn sight. I blended in with the others in line and was totally unprepared to be looking into the face I had been so curious about. It was handsome, long aristocratic nose, wavy hair peppered artistically with grey. Prince or pauper, I knew not which, but I was totally taken in by his good looks.

My new understanding utterly eclipsed what had been formerly clinical skepticism, with what ease he must have practiced his dark deceipts.

Prill had disappeared without notice.

At the large Moyer Presbyterian plot in the cemetery in Pleasantville, not a word was said, sadness overcame us all and "earth to earth, ashes to ashes" was the common destiny of all. The small circle of mourners in black, shoulder to shoulder, seemed to be nodding to the unseen presence above, the same small group who had attended the funeral here of Uncle Clovis..

This was followed by a luncheon at the church, prepared by those loyal Lutheran ladies.

No one spoke and Carlie's friend quickly lead her out the door an away to her earned solitude. She seemed immune to the present world surrounding her.

One of the lessons came to mind, from the Book of Job. "but now mine eye seeth thee. Wherefore I abhor myself and repent in dust and ashes". Iit was time for Frank to take his rest with his family in the family plot in Pleasantville.

Chapter 15

Things Settle Down

Things had settled down in the last two weeks. It was quiet, to everyone's relief. Carlie would be getting chemotherapy treatments to shrink the tumor that was found and was expecting surgery on it in the fall. Grace and Prill were planning to accompany her to her treatments in Philly. Carlie was unable to drive, due to her new medication, and the company was welcome.

I was working in my new garden, planting the full grown, end of season assortment all by myself. I welcomed the activity. We were planning a garden club for winter, to include all of the women of the church. I personally hoped we would do a lot more visiting of places such as Longwood gardens, than actually of working in one. My back was killing me. I ordered some new lawn chairs, as the first meeting would be here in my garden in Sea Isle.

The phone rang, waking me out of my reverie. It was Robert. He had just had a call from Carlie and it seemed urgent. She wanted him to come right out to the green farm

building she had just moved into, due to necessity. It was so unlike her to make any requests of the church, he agreed to come at once. "You can bring your wife if you like."

Robert suggested he bring his mother instead, if she didn't mind. She didn't.

I met him there in less than an hour. She rushed into the house, sat us down, and said "Can you tell me what this is all about?" she asked as she placed a large legal envelope in Robert's hands. I knew what it was by the look on his face. His contract, appearing at last. "Why did we owe you money? This was in the safe, I've been going through Frank's papers, and I found this strange one. It's a mortgage on the house next door."

Robert took his time answering. "Carlie, I believe Frank was trying to help Scott pay for classes at Harvard. He also wanted to move Uncle Clovis into someplace close to care for him. He borrowed money from me to buy the house next door. Things just got piled up one on top of another, and the whole darn mess unraveled. He was shuffling his money around to do both."

"But why is Scott's name on the deed"? This answer had to be diplomatic. "He was probably just there at the signing, something simple like that", I quickly responded. "But it's also on the deed for Clovis's home." She probably was not fully aware of divorce laws. It seems he was going to separate after all. I really thought we shouldn't answer any more questions and so did Robert, without some serious discussion, due to her condition.

"Not right now, Carlie", Robert said. I'd like you to know one thing. You're not in this alone. You've got a whole church behind you," he said as he folded an arm around her..

"We'll see it through all the way to the end".

We found ourselves beside the old safe in Frank's house and the door was wide open. Robert shifted over to see inside. He pulled out a wad of fifty dollar bills, along with some twenty dollar denominations. They were bundled into rubber bands. Apparently repairs were a lucrative business

The whole wall of reserve she had built up was staring to break down. Then the dam broke.

Carlie's cell phone rang. I assumed it was Scott. She simply said "Yes, of course, I'm here at the house."

Her next statement was a surprise. She said to Robert "Would you please move your car, then call the police".

"Pastor. I can't go on not knowing---what has been going on?"

She weeped aloud, "and what am I going to do with these" as she reached inside and grabbed these pittiful notes to her ample bosom.

My questions to myself was, how obligated am I to see the results carried out to the letter of the law?"

The answer didn't require much of a decision at all. "What would be the whole point of this mission if I were to observe the object of a lifetime of love and training stealing a document from the safe of another persons, criminal though he might have been."

Robert glanced at me out of his left eye and knew he'd better close the safe door until official witnesses were present. A mother's relief, at least this mother's relief.

We exited the residence.

Chapter 16

At the Green Farm House

Robert and I waited at the front of the lane to Frank's farm house. My son called the police from there and asked that they proceed cautiously, a woman's life might be in danger. We watched a dirty white van slowly climb the lane and followed the squad car, which arrived quickly.

The white van was parked in front of the ugly eyesore, which had still not been properly repaired. When we saw the police escort Scott from the house, we rushed inside. Carlie was safe, but grief stricken. I held her in my arms, and we went to her little room to pick up her bag, which was still unpacked. I put her prescriptions inside.

We talked Carlie into moving to my home in Sea Isle for the night, and told her we'd talk later. I just wanted her out of there. As she settled into my Town Car she exclaimed, "What could happen to me next?"

Robert followed behind us all the way. Once settled safely inside, we prayed a prayer of safe delivery, safe from further injuries and that justice would follow. We settled Carlie into a comfortable chair with a cup of tea and allowed her tranquilizers to take effect.

First of all, though, she wished to speak out about the events of the evening. "I knew it had to be Scott once I saw that the Barretta had been removed from the gun case. It was the only one Scott was comfortable with. He and his father practiced behind the garage whenever they could. There'll be some shells there to compare with the ones found near the crime scene."

"it dawned on me that Scott intended me to take the blame. It was too easy, since I was also familiar with the Barretta, pretty good with it actually. He just didn't know I would ever, ever shoot Frank. He knew it was my week off and that I might not have an alibi. That's the part that hurts the most."

"I had been to see a divorce lawyer. She suggested that if I couldn't afford a private detective, I should follow Frank whenever I could, it might provide something useful.

Well, I did just that. I saw a while van parked on the other side of the cabin right before the shooting occurred.

Once I saw Scott appear in it, as he did tonight, I knew he'd driven down from Harvard in it, and didn't arrive by plane the way the news media suggested. Scott was always too smart for his own good".

"I just wish Frank knew him the way I did. I watched him become more selfish and non-caring as time went on. It didn't surprise me that Scott was no longer in school when I called to tell them about his father, it was almost a year since he'd been enrolled. I guess Frank found out the same thing."

"He must have used the money Frank sent him to buy the van, the van that helped him kill his father."

"Should I call a lawyer, he is still my son?" "No, dear" I answered, "you don't have to, he's over eighteen and definitely not in college".

"He killed the only man I ever loved, I'll have to think hard on that one."

"Poor Frank, he wanted his only son to have everything he never had, like the rich folks on the hill had."

I thought silently of Prill, who Frank thought of as one of those privileged few, and how easily he had eased himself into a life he'd neither created, nor deserved. That, after being raised in Back Neck, was hard to swallow. We would not dwell on that now, however. Talk about the apple not falling far from the tree.

After Robert left, I led her to the small room downstairs that his father had used, with TV and powder room. She didn't need to know that either. That room held so many precious memories. I had better leave quickly.

Sleep well child, and peace attend thee! "Thank you so much Mrs. Peterson" she said as her drugged eyes closed. She was in dreamland, where reality couldn't reach her.

What was nagging in the back of my head? Some unconscious prick from that location lead me to get out of my four poster bed. I slid into my old fashioned mules, went to the door, and put the deadbolt on from the inside. There, that was better. Sleep followed shortly.

Chapter 17

Then Came the Morning

Promptly the next morning two plain clothes detectives appeared at my door. Probably the news of her tumor had been explained to them, they were very solemn and concerned. I escorted them into my kitchen and hoped they would keep the conversation short and to the point. They did.

Carlie mostly reported her information of the previous evening They took prolific notes. She held up quite well in spite of this intrusion into what I had hoped would be a quiet morning and a restful recovery. Pipe dreams, I thought, it was too late for that.

They had no new information, had found nothing of value as yet, and were proceeding cautiously. They were keeping options open, I thought, knowing the condition of her mind, and that she was their only witness. I stressed that we now had motive, I don't think they took me seriously, however. Scott was entitled to a lawyer, if he wanted one.

Luckily, I alone would have access to the phone, hers was packed away into a compartment of her suitcase, which was not easily accessible, with the volume lowered.

This in case that "one" phone call arrived.

They left shortly and we were both relieved. They left their cards behind should we remember anything of value.

"Where do I go from here." Carlie said. "I have family in upper New York state, which I haven't seen in a while." "No need to think at all" I said, "Let's just go by your prognosis. You have family here too, and a room as long as you like. Your doctors are all around here or Pennsylvania"

There would be a trial, and I hoped she'd take as little part in it as possible. I prayed she'd keep her mind on her recovery, but I also knew she was in good hands, God's hands. His plans for us were perfect in every way.

It was time time to think of a lawyer for Carlie, one who would take her place on the stand. One who could withstand pressure would be needed. Perhaps Robert knew of someone. Life hadn't prepared me for this one.

Carlie as well as Scott had access to the Barretta, and she was skilled with it, as well as he. She herself had admitted this to both of us the night before. I wish the police knew her as well as we did! How could we convey this to them?

That afternoon I called Grace. "Did it work? You know, cheering up Prill by taking her out to dinner and a move."

"Bring her over her, I'm a good cook and I'll rent a comedy for my big screen TV". We did just that in the evening, enjoyed a gourmet, non alcoholic dinner, had a great desert and watched a movie appropriate mild and uplifting for her mood.

Carlie really relaxed in the comfortable Town Car on the way home. As I pulled up into my driveway, I was thinking I might need some help getting this large woman into the house. I was dialing Robert, thinking dumb move Angie, when she started mumbling something, something of interest that made me put my ear to her mouth, She was sayins,

"In the spare tire, Frank, you always kept it there, no one ever knew."
Robert picked up his cell phone and I said "You'd better get over here real quick".
It's a whole new development, and I have a feeling I might know exactly what it means."

Chapter 18

Back Home Again in Sea Isle

The following days were quiet again back in our little shore community. I had been in the throes of preparation for my garden party, to show off the results of my gardening exuberance. It did indeed look well. I decided I'd let my imagination run more than a little off course. It happened some days.

It had all come together at last. The garden was spectacular, with the help of Luis, my neighbor, we created a dramatic memory to my late husband using the hostas and myrtle he had planted as a focal point. It was colorful and lively. A great place to kick off plans for a gardening club for the faithful church members, and it certainly lifted my spirits.

My son was there, naturally, along with some of the old guard from Bethlehem Lutheran church. Luis had set up card tables and the conversation went as follows: "I half expect Frank to show up in his truck with Uncle Clovis alongside" was heard from a few of the assorted flock.

I was looking for the appearance of the pizza delivery van, when my glance fell on the sight of Carlie, who was still staying with me. Some look on her face totally gripped my attention.

She was completely wrapped up in the world of Chloe's kitten she was presently adoring, but it was the look on her face that stunned me. It was, yes, the look of the proverbial "cat that ate the canary"! That look, yes, it was a happy look as if a plan had succeeded which had been skillfully plotted.

Why had we been so blinded by our own feelings, mostly the desire to see an outcome that appealed to our desire to see a happy ending we could sympathize with! Yes, the fact was that she could have been behind this gruesome act, as well as her son Scott. The possibility existed that either could have done it. We knew very little of the personalities behind both suspects, we merely preferred one above the other. This fact had nagged in the back of my mind all along. I had to leave quickly and find out for myself.

I whispered a brief message to Luis to inform Robert, then grabbed my purse from the hall closet. Some instinct made me check my wallet. Not to my surprise, credit cards and more than a little cash were missing. Add cunning to the list, Angellica.

I jumped into the Town Car and left, not slowing down until I saw the spirals of the court house, where I turned in and found an empty spot in the adjacent jail. I ran inside to a drab grey/green room, void of any pictures at all, went through security and to the information desk I was surrounded by correction officers, who wondered what crime I had committed, or what low life I was visiting, and found I was very late.. There were minutes left to Saturday visiting hours. Once again, in an atmosphere of "three hots and a cot" my stubborn nature prevailed and I found myself being lead through thick plastic doors by guards to a row of cubicles and then at the top of a head which I thought might be Scott.

I had never met him. I was still talking to the top of a blond head, pleading my case. "Please believe me, I know that you're innocent. Only one person could have placed that gun in the tire of your van. She'd seen it done many times in the past by your father." Slowly that face lifted itself, and my wish came true at last. However, it was not that person, a younger, scared Frank that I expected, but my son Robert, betrayed by life,. although, unlike Robert, Scott was visibly crushed under the weight of it all. "Please help me , Lord."

"Don't talk -- I'll be here on Monday. It's Pastors visiting day. Your Dad's pastor is my son and we'll bring a lawyer, then you can talk". I was ushered out in haste, but I'd gotten my message across, in any case. How could I have been so dumb!

Monday came and went. Robert went out there alone. It would be difficult to find the right defense attorney. He (Robert) first of all would have to confirm my story. I don't think he quite believed me, at first, that is. He came around to my thinking after some days of objective refection on the matter. The fact that Carlie was becoming unraveled, and very quickly at that, was the most convincing factor to change his decision, that and the missing cards. Our first duty was to get care for her, and Robert used his influence in the community to do so.

My son, happily, was once again thinking like his father and secured access to Frank's safe. I knew he was scrupulous enough to wait for Scott's approval to remove it to a safe place until he (Scott) would eventually find himself the beneficiary of a host of properties, some of which were unrecognizable to any of us.

That poor boy. His only parents had been his downfall. I should have remembered Dawn's admission that Scott couldn't make a move without his father's approval. Well he would have to learn how, and real fast!

Chapter 19

The Mind of a Sleuth

So how had I come to this complete reversal in the main character of this vicious murder? I needed to get back into the routine of my simpler life, to restore it to some sense of normality. The answer of course, was my quilt making.

My party was days away, and Luis seemed to have a good grasp of what needed to be done. I headed upstairs to my quilt room, where my pieces were already arrayed on my work table. It was a hiatus of colors, the more the merrier to my thinking.

While my hands were busy arranging the small squares into a soothing pattern of pale pinks, yellows and soft assorted greens, suddenly a pink checkered square became a green farm house, a yellow strip became the city of Cambridge and my small scissors became a dusty white van, moving steadily back and forth between the two. I took this six hour trip steadily for about a half hour, saying to myself. "This is all wrong."

In review, Scott took this trip in his van, down from Harvard to the green farm house, parked beside it, called his father's cell phone to tell him of the destruction, used his key, (supposing he had one) to remove the gun from its cabinet, went outside, and waited in the shadows to shoot him. He then drove from my pink checkered square to the yellow and white square, then took a plane when he heard the news.

No, this was not a plan for a young man who could not make a move without his father's blessings, as Dawn had correctly (to my thinking) deduced.

Robert had told me that Scott had a chance to grab a ride back to Harvard, which was the current story of why he had missed the funeral. I believe there were early awakenings of how the facts were stacking up and that van made it down here to south Jersey when a decision was made to move down here and defend himself.

Once I realized that Carlie had lied about seeing the van, I knew the plan all along had been to break into the house and get to the gun cabinet. The rest was easy.

I called Carlie's employment, who verified that she was back in her home by ten o'clock in the morning on the day in question.

The police found the gun in the spare tire after a thorough search, which must have been placed there by Carlie in the few minutes in which she'd found herself alone. Not a bad plan at all, but it was still a theory at best.

At this moment I was pulled away and back into the present by a call for help from Luis and promptly answered the SOS. The sleuth was tucked away for the moment, and I headed downstairs.

//////////////////////////////////////

Chapter 20

//////////////////////////////////////

About the Last and Final Stage

Poor Scott had lost both mother and father, but I sensed it was the beginning of a relationship between him, Prill, Gracie, and me... He showed no desire to return to Harvard to resume studies, he was simply happy to be out of jail, no not happy but relieved.

As for my attempt at a garden party, it will go down in the annals as my worst party ever. To recap, Luis had relayed my message to Robert, and it was the beginning of Carlie's quick descent into madness. Everyone witnessed it. Her eyes turned red, her bridge fell out of her mouth and she kept screaming expletives about her husband. Her large size compounded the image.

Someone had the good sense to contact Bridgeton Hospital, (New Jersey's attempt to combat mental illness on the sixth floor), and they came promptly for an evaluation. These beautiful professionals handled it expertly. I assume they had handled it far too many times. She was safely out of my home when I returned and I slept soundly that night.

My last coherent thought before I entered dreamland was, yes --- Dawn's last statement "Scott could never make a move without his father's permission" turned out to be prophetic. It was there all the time and I couldn't connect the dots, hearsay, perhaps but correct hearsay.

I planned to investigate Scott's heritage. I'm sure he'll turn out to be a love child of Frank's reckless youth. I hope so, in any case.

As for Ruth, my daughter in law, she was no longer leaving her son's future up to chance, but was renewing her certification with the state of New Jersey's teaching program.

I myself was planning to join a guided tour of New Orleans. I wonder if you can still ride the Streetcar named Desire for five cents, and oh those cute boutiques and Antoins of course.

I had lunched at Docks with Prill, and couldn't help myself by saying, "You know of course it was you he loved all along." She nodded sadly and assented to my words.

I kept the words to myself, as I bit my tongue, " and that was his wife and she killed him." Her future had crashed, but I knew she could handle it, whatever would follow.

I knew that with certainty. At least she'd keep most of her money.

Robert seemed no different, but I had a new respect for him. His calm nature, strength of purpose and desire to do the 'right thing' in any case, cemented my confidence in him.

How proud Rob would have been.

We'd found out at the cemetery the truth of the relationship from Frank's family.

Scott had been the product of a previous illicit relationship before he had married Carlie, as I 'd hoped, and her jealousy of Scott had always existed.

"And the Lord turned the captivity of Job when he prayed for his friends and gave him twice as much as he had before. .Job lived an hundred and forty years and saw his sons and his son's sons every four generations." His poor wife was busy replacing the children he'd lost.

I had finished the bible study of Job